FOR THE LOVE OF A PSYCHO

VICTORIA WOLF

PAGE PUBLISHING
Conneaut Lake, PA

First originally published by Page Publishing 2023

ISBN 979-8-88793-839-4 (pbk)
ISBN 979-8-88793-836-3 (digital)

Printed in the United States of America

Contents

Introduction v
Prologue and a Warning...vii
Who Is Not Normal? 1
What Culture?... 6
A Belief System or What? 12
Who Is Wrong? 18
Is Hate Safe?... 26
Who Are You? 33
What Law and Order?... 42
Are Feelings the Truth?... 48
Epilogue.. 55

Introduction

I have written this book hoping to add a little bit to the subject regarding general abuse of women in the world. I also wrote this because I believe that despite all the statistics, there is a much greater number of women who suffer in silence at the hands of a certain kind of man. My story consists of three parts.

The first part is a story in verse. It is a story about Jeffry, the psycho who is stomping through various lives, leaving death and devastation behind him. He is completely convinced that he is right in what he is doing and that all his victims deserved what they get. He is, also, convinced that by his mere existence, he has more rights than other people.

The second part is the story carried by the Poster Girl, which represents reality. Her posters bring forward the gruesome reality of the magnitude of abuse of women. This part is based on facts from the United Nations and various other renowned sources and can all be easily found and confirmed on the Internet.

The third story is in very broad strokes a psychological analysis of the psychopath given by the Good Doctor in his articles. Again, this part is based on current findings by various authors and on my personal experience. I started writing it when I was more or less housebound because I had a stalker for three years, who wished me only harm. During these endless hours of living in fear, I got very little help from anyone. I tried to not let him change my life, but alas, I lost that battle and, after three years, moved at night and in secrecy to get away from him. Today, over ten years later, I still make sure I know who is ringing my doorbell and whose car is parked in my street.

I have no intention of making this a scientific book, a textbook, or a psychological study. It is just my story, and all is just based on how I see it and how I feel about the whole subject. It's not an anti-man book. I have a son, a husband, and a father, whom I love very much. It is a book only about men who are psychopaths and their victims.

Prologue and a Warning

> **About 47,000 women and girls worldwide were killed in 2020. This number went to 50,000 in 2022. This means that 137 women are killed every day by their partners or family members. One woman is killed every ten minutes according to the latest UN figures.**

I n most cultures, most people will consider that it is not fair when a strong person attacks or torments a weaker or more vulnerable person. "Pick on someone your own size" is a saying that is widely understood, and so is the fact that only a lesser human being will instead of protecting the weak look for a vulnerable human to abuse.

It needs to be said that *vulnerable* means "people with a weakness, which can be physical, emotional, or mental," but it is also very important to note that vulnerable people are not wimps or some sort of a "born to be victimized" human subcategory.

The people who live to victimize the vulnerable are psychos, psychopaths, sociopaths, people who suffer from borderline personality disorders, or whatever you wish to call them. Their secret is that they are made in a different way from normal people. They exist in every walk of life and in every country across the world. They all have a certain number of common characteristics since their brains seem to be wired differently in comparison to an average human brain. Their brain waves, when measured in a laboratory setting, have a specific reaction, which is not found among the non-psychopathic population. Their brains show a deficit in the emotional processing of events around them. So their brains seem to be wired differently to most of our brains, and this fact, in turn, makes them see the world in a much different way than most of humanity. Their brain wiring, and the way they see the world, also warps their thinking and disfigures their instincts. Many of them create their own world in their minds where they feel comfortable. In their world, justice, law, love, relationships, etc. are all based on how the psycho thinks they ought to be.

Unfortunately, they live in our world where they don't feel comfortable because all our rules are different. It is "in our world" where they hurt very many people because they play by the rules they set themselves. For instance, a Psycho Vulgaris who is also a pedophile plays by the rules of his warped world, where he proclaims that children want to have sex with adults and where rationalization, denial, justification, and complete lack of empathy are used to set the rules. He also knows that his behavior is not acceptable in our wider society, so he hides who he is while blaming society for "being prejudice" and "making" him pretend he is someone else. He does not see himself as an abuser; rather, most of them will say that the children participated gladly and will go to great lengths to explain how they only feel love for the children. I am fully aware that they do not change their sexual preference for children no matter what happens to them and that there is no therapy for pedophilia. I also, unfortunately, don't belong to the group of people who think they need to be helped or rehabilitated. In a society like ours, I strongly believe that all existing finite resources for providing help should be directed toward the victims.

One of the first clinicians who studied psychopaths was P. Pinel. This was in the early nineteenth century. He considered them as people who do worse things than "ordinary evil men." His contemporaries titled them "morally insane," and all saw them as evil. Some people believe that there is a concrete evil entity like the Devil stalking humans; other see evil only as a part of the human psyche. I personally do not know why it exists at all when it is a completely useless trait, which, in the end, does not bring any lasting solutions even to the evildoer. H. Cleckley published a book in 1941 called *The Mask of Sanity*. This is one of the most important books published on this subject, and it kicked off serious research into this problem. The goal was to find an instrument that would measure psychopathy correctly. The existing clinical tests did not work when psychopathy was concerned because psychos seemed to be able to complete them presenting themselves in whichever light they wanted to. These tests relied on self-reporting, and the psychos learned very quickly how to *use* them in their favor. It was Robert Hare who developed an instrument that is used today to clinically differentiate between psychopaths and *others* and called it the Psychopathy Checklist. It is used very widely and is excellent in diagnosing psychopaths. It is especially useful to parole boards, as it can be reliably used to predict repeat offenders. The book in which Robert Hare discusses his findings and conclusions on the subject of psychopaths was first published in New York in 1995 and is called *Without Conscience*. It is a great read, and in it, you can find the *key symptoms of psychopathy* explained. According to Dr. Robert Hare, psychopathy is a is a syndrome and a cluster of the following behaviors:

Emotional/Interpersonal Social Deviance

1. Glib and superficial
2. Impulsive
3. Egocentric and grandiose
4. Poor behavior controls
5. Lack of remorse or guilt
6. Need for excitement
7. Lack of empathy
8. Lack of responsibility
9. Deceitful and manipulative
10. Early behavior problems
11. Shallow emotions
12. Adult antisocial behavior

Where a normal person sees the need to help and protect, they see prey. They are the utilitarians of this world who look for the vulnerable to use and abuse to make themselves feel powerful, to feel good about themselves, and to feel victorious. It is not only about feelings. They are out to steal, to live at your expense, and to take whatever they can get their hands on. They are the users and abusers, with strong narcissistic tendencies, which are reflected in their self-centered existence. They are the people who cause hurt and harm to everyone they get close to, and they do this over and over again because their *feelings of victory* last only for a short time. They are mostly men who feel no remorse or guilt for the things they have done. Ted Bundy, the serial killer who confessed to murdering thirty-seven women, though many believe he could have killed twice that many, said about guilt: "It is a mechanism we use to control people and it is very unhealthy—it is an illusion and does terrible things to our bodies."

They know they are different to the majority. To cover up this fact, they learn early on in life to mimic acceptable behavior that they see around them so they would fit in. Often, they are CEOs, generals, presidents, and all other kinds of successful people, but quite a few, or better said, most of them are just abusers. There is the *criminal psychopath* who engages in lawless behavior, and then, as Dr. Robert Hare said, "There is the SUB-CRIMINAL category of psychopaths that will never go to prison and that appears to function relatively reasonably." These kinds of psychos cause very wide harm within the general population by leaving a trail of abused people. They resort to emotional abuse, philandering, lying, cheating, stealing, and bullying and are unfortunately very often not incarcerated or even fined for their heartless deeds. The jailbirds, killers, gangsters, and crooks are just the tip of the iceberg—a frightening thought.

Some people call them psychological vampires, while others claim they have no soul, but one thing they all have in common is that there is no cure for this condition. Psychiatry realized that they manipulate their therapists quite well and learn from psychotherapy how to get around the *system*. There were various attempts to prevent this manipulation of the therapist. For instance, they tried changing to a different therapist every few months so the therapist would not be *ensnared* by the psycho. Nothing really worked; the ones who chose the route of crime reoffended regularly; the ones who were paroled went back to doing whatever it was they were in jail for in the first place. Inmates who score high on Hare's Psychopathy Checklist are four to eight times more likely to be recidivists than those with a low score.

The Psycho Vulgaris cannot change, no therapy works for them, and none of them in their self-centered and narcissistic existence don't really wish to bother with it. They have no intention of changing, nor do they in their grandiosity see why they should. Psychopathy is not the same as psychosis; they don't hallucinate, and their thinking, though evil, is functional. It is not a mental illness like schizophrenia or the manic–depressive disorder but a combination of developmental and genetic conditions—they are made that way. Because of the differences found between psychopaths and the general population in the way their brain functions, it is logical to conclude that psychopathy has a physiological component, which may be hereditary or caused by early brain injury. It is generally accepted that the *nurture* in his life determines in large part how the syndrome manifests itself and how it is expressed in his behavior. Unfortunately, children can exhibit and keep exhibiting throughout their life all the characteristics of a psychopath. This early psychopathy seems not to be connected to the quality of the upbringing of a child. Although their family life may be stable or unstable, psychopaths first appear in family court on average at the age of fourteen.

There are different estimates of the percentages of psychopaths in any population (anywhere from 2 to 5 percent), but most estimates show that men are in the majority. If there are eight billion people on planet Earth and if only 1 percent of them belong to the category of Psycho Vulgaris, there are eighty million psychopaths wondering around looking for victims right now. There are various theories of nature vs. nurture, and some scientists believe that this condition is somehow connected to one of the main male genes, the MAOA *warrior gene*, which is on the x chromosome. The *warrior gene* is a glamourous name for aggression, and I guess I would prefer if it was named something less *noble* sounding.

An average psycho hides who he is; he maneuvers people to satisfy his own needs and, while using people, will show an amazing lack of empathy. It makes sense that the one's that victimize do not feel the victim's pain. Empathy is the main thing that keeps normal people from torturing or causing pain to others. The average psycho has a very highly developed skill of *reading* other people yet usually very little if any inclination toward introspection (reading oneself). Knowing where to press other people's *buttons* is a condition without which successful manipulating of others is not possible; it also allows them to keep long-term control over a person. They are often very cunning and can be very intelligent.

Dr. Martha Stout in her book, *The Sociopath Next Door*, says that conscience is a late evolutionary development in humans. We seemed to have had, according to her, millions of years of evolution, which led us to our *seventh* sense as she called it. Conscience was first the subject of theology and later of science. We can see it developing in our children as they slowly leave the *I am the center of the universe* phase to a more socialized phase, when they understand that *sharing is caring*. I sometimes get the impression that psychos stopped developing emotionally at the age of one. They remained the center of the universe, never developed a sense for others, and never developed a sense of morality as most people know it. They can develop a warped series of rules based on the laws made by them. For instance, the BTK killer in an interview when asked if he raped his victims answered with indignation that he would never stoop that low. He killed them for sure, but rape never; rape is for lowlifes.

If you have not experienced a relationship with a psycho, you may have heard someone sharing how "he changed" once they got married. A psycho will know when to turn on the charm of a predator, and once he has got you, he will change into who he really is. Very quickly one can see that that there are two aspects of his personality, and the confusion he creates with changing from one role to the other keeps "the chosen one" by his side. She keeps on waiting for the "nice him" to come back, the one she has fallen for in the first place. She does not realize that this confusion he causes will turn into her obsessive need to understand him, and while this is going on, she will pay no attention to her own feelings or needs. She keeps on expecting him to change, not realizing that she is wanting the impossible because no more than she can grow a second head can he turn into a good man.

She ends up abused with a huge low self-esteem problem, without the money she had, often without a job, and with no friends because he had her alienate all of them so that she, his victim, would have no support system.

The woman I have just described is the lucky one because she kept her life! Many are not so lucky and meet their end at the hands of the psycho. If you ever recognize one, just run in the opposite direction, and do not stop till you are safe. Don't pick up the phone, don't talk to him, and do not have any contact with him so that he cannot crawl his way into your life.

He will not change back to being a nice guy. That was the role he played while *charming* you. When he feels he has you hooked, you then become his possession, which in turn he will proclaim worthless. This is when he shows his true face.

THE WARNING

1. You must leave, and you'll remove the necessary component; his aggression will lose meaning when he has no opponent.
2. He won't stop to torture every soul he can catch; he needs to destroy you, the one that's his match.
3. While he performs his deeds, which are gory and gritty, you will give away your power if you feel any pity.

4. You will be discarded once you have been used; so ask yourself the following, before you get too confused:

1. Does he have opinions and take a firm stand on many an issue he does not understand?
2. Does he find it funny if you are scared at night? Does he always, but always, have to be right?
3. Must he be the strongest and always the best? Did he ever mention kindness as a true manly quest?
4. In order to function, must he feel superior, and to keep this illusion, will he kiss any posterior?
5. Did he ask you to give him your heart on a platter, and does he nurture the notion that feelings don't matter?
6. Does he take your money and act as if he was younger than you, though he's fifty-five and you are thirty-two?
7. Is it always your fault, and are you the one to blame that he's never achieved any fortune or fame?
8. Is he the one who will take, only take, and after taking it all, will he still ask for the cake?
9. Does he often scare you and lead you to sorrow? If his middle name is *misery*, there's no sunny tomorrow.
10. Do you know that his inner darkness and his desolation are the perfect ingredients for your own annihilation?

If there are seven yeses to the questions asked above, he is a user and a psycho, and there is no love. Do not expect him to change; he is made that way, his brain is wired in a certain way, and besides, in his endless narcissism, he thinks he is wonderful and sees no need to change. His nature is close to the nature of a spider, so do not be the fly in his web!

HOW DO SPIDERS THINK

Come into my world said the spider to the fly
Come sit on my lap, of course you won't die

Do not be afraid, I'll make you feel nice
I know you will see I am a bug with no vice

When you feel at peace all cozy and trusting
I'll caress and woo you and then leave you lusting

You'll want me so much, but I'll not be near
So stricken by yearning you'll consider me dear

I will kiss your pinkie and stroke your sweet cheek
I'll put on airs and graces of a man that is weak

I'll tell you my troubles, how I never had a shield,
Once your heart starts bleeding my power is sealed

I'll not tell the truth; my truth will cause pain
I will make the effort because I will gain

Our romance will last while I digest part of you
The fact is I'm feeding, and you don't have a clue.

I'll swallow your eyes and you'll still count on me
I'll describe the world you won't need to see

When it is too late, you'll know things aren't right
It won't matter then, you're too weak for flight

I am a spider you are the fly, eating you is my way
If I mentioned love, it was just so you'd stay

You were naïve enough to so easily believe
That I loved you madly and would never leave

I did speak the truth, I cherished you as a food
And while warm and wiggling you were very good

In a way you were right, I am not going away
You are the one to go, I am the one to stay

Now all I need to do is flush your remains away
And at my front door all will hear me say

Come into my world you pretty little fly, don't worry
There is no trap, of course you won't die

Who Is Not Normal?

I AM THE OLD FART

I am Jeffry, the Old Fart, the one that is strange; I knew being happy
    was out of my range
I did everything I could my dreams never to get; I need to be miser-
    able I must never forget
No one ever loved me because they all knew of the badness I've done
    and the bad things I'll do
I won't fall in love; I just could not stand it; she would take my soul
    in an instant or even demand it
I'd be happier living with a frog in the gutter; with a frog, there'd be
    peace and my heart wouldn't flutter
When I am all alone, there is no reason to worry, if I let her in, she'll
    wreck my life in a hurry
My fear is so great it is ruining my health; women operate undercover
    they all exercise stealth
I keep thinking of her—it must be black magic; do I dare love her
    when our end will be tragic
Oh, Doctor, Doctor, it is a seriously bad condition—do something
    now; I am approaching demolition
Surgery is the solution, please remove my brain and my heart; and I'll
    be happy alone, living like an Old Fart
I'll gladly go under the good doctor's knife; I won't think I won't feel
    what a wonderful life

Like an Old Fart, I am safe that is how things stand; things don't have
to mean much if peace is at hand
It is so rewarding to live with no worry and no fear; a free man at last,
I don't want anyone near
They say love will belong to the one that dares; any Old Fart will tell
you that no Old Fart cares

DEAR DOCTOR

Dear Doctor, I listened to Jeffry talk about himself so badly; I felt
sorry for him, I will help him gladly
I thought I'd invite him for lunch when we could have a nice chat; a
sad lonely grandpa, it should not be like that
When I asked him to visit and offered some company, his whole face
changed, and he growled at me
Dear Doctor, what happened, I did not mean to offend; I just wanted
to be nice so his hurt heart could mend

DOC'S SCIENCE

Listen to me, girl, you must learn the science; with a man like him,
it's always a deadly alliance
He is a Psycho Vulgaris, he'll change at a whim; by offering kindness,
you've only upset him
He is not a good man; he will cause lots of harm; once you are his, he
will switch off the charm
I wrote an article, which you should read; do you know you can be
punished for performing a good deed

THE ARTICLE

One of the most intriguing characteristics of the psychopath is their benign "Dr. Jekyll" appearance. Depending on the scale of psychopathy, the Psycho Vulgaris can be anything from a CEO of a big company to a Wall Street trader or from a mass murderer to a serial killer.

For instance, Albert Fish, a gentle-looking grandfather, was a serial killer and a cannibal. He lured children to their death and then cooked them and ate them.

> I put strips of bacon on each cheek of his behind
> and put them in the oven. After about two hours,
> it was nice and brown and cooked through. I
> never ate any roast turkey that tasted half as good.

While awaiting trial, he, with his eyes full of tears, said, "Am still worried about my children, you would think they would come to visit their old dad in jail, but they haven't."

Fish had killed about fifteen children and mutilated about another eighty. He was married and had six children of his own ranging from the age of twenty-one to thirty-five when he was finally arrested. All up to the day he was caught, he was considered by his neighbors to be a mild and shy but decent neighbor. Even when he was left to live alone, the worst thing people may have called him was *an Old Fart*, which is so far away from what he really was, which is a psycho, a serial killer of children, and a cannibal.

Wondering how come it takes so long to find and stop a serial killer, I realized that one of the reasons are our own expectations. Society approves of the average, and since it is a fact that psychos learn to mimic the *majority's* actions and reactions, it is difficult to see *the monster* behind a carefully built, benign facade. Also, monsters in human form do not necessarily look evil. On the contrary, they look, walk, and talk like most of us. Mimicry is their tool for survival, a tool for approaching his victims, and it is a prerequisite of any serial killer if he is to become serial. They hide in public by being just an *average Joe* as this is their means of concealment. Naturally, if people knew or could tell who they were, they would have a problem in *obtaining* victims, they so desperately need to prove their *strength* and *power* to themselves and the world.

> # In the Us a woman is raped every 6 minutes, and a woman is battered every 15 seconds. (Rainn 2022)

So the question of who is normal is not my concern here, and I will not even attempt to answer it. But it seems glaringly obvious that psychopaths are not normal. Who does the things they do? Who eats children and rapes, tortures, and maims anyone they can get their hands on? Surely, not *normal people*, not the ones within *the average* spread along Gausses line of probability. Psychos fit in among the average through imitating the people they are surrounded by, while in secrecy, committing the worst crimes. They are only *normal* in the legal sense of this word, i.e., they know exactly what they are doing, and they know right from wrong, but they just do not give a toss and want to do whatever it is they are doing over and over.

Because of their extremely shallow emotions and their complete lack of empathy, psychos can learn the moral codes of their environment. Then they pretend they have a conscience as a part of their mimicry. They learn what moral norms are by observing others, and to them, *morals* are a purely cognitive exercise. They don't interiorize any moral codes, and they do not attach any feelings to them. They don't feel *a conscience*, and they do not feel good or bad about what they do in a moral sense. They feel no satisfaction when they do the right thing, nor guilt when they do the wrong thing. They know what acceptable behavior in the society they live in is, so they know when they are doing the unacceptable thing. They know, but they don't feel either way about it; they just don't care.

Whether they care or not, the subconscious mind registers our actions. It registers if we are doing the right thing or the wrong thing according to our inner *judge*. This is not a conscious process but will influence our self-esteem, which is very important for a general sense of being worthy, and it raises and falls depending on our actions and on what we *allow* others to do to us. So our actions have significant inner reactions that further determine how we feel and what we do.

People tend to trust others with similar traits to themselves. The psycho, by mimicking *averageness* at first glance, fits in enough to expand his hunting ground. By fitting in, he is not looking for a friend, and he is not a sad lonely old man without an agenda. On the contrary, taking away your well-being, even your life, is his agenda, and sustaining the image of "the average Jo" is his *way* to obtaining his goal. Is this normal? Not at all; psychopaths seem like everyone else, only superficially. Inside, they are uncaring monsters to a greater or a lesser degree. They are legally normal—they choose what to do, then they execute it, and they know it is wrong, but they do not care.

What Culture?

THE TOUGH MACHO MAN

My name is Jeffry, and I am a tough, macho drunk; a hardworking,
    hard-playing man, not a punk
I quite often swear, and I love to curse; every picked-up resentment I
    will cherish and nurse
Girls tell me I always make the same stupid mistake of wanting to eat
    and keep the same cake
Though my smile can be fake and my words not sincere, I think I'll
    get far just by playing it by ear
As the macho man, I'll know no defeat, as a great macho man I will
    beat her and cheat
A woman can't be trusted, a man she'll desert like my own mother
    did when I was only a kid
One day I met the one "that was meant to be," she was very pretty
    and seemed just happy to be
I asked her to marry me, said I would be kind; her answer was "yes,"
    love has made her blind
But I knew that once she was in my embrace, I'll cheat, and I'll steal,
    and I'll slap her fair face
I'll hit her again if she utters a wrong word; she's a stupid woman not
    meant to be heard
Once I manage to ruin her very pretty face; I will simply move on to
    enjoy another's embrace

One gray rainy morning, I went to see if our old house was still
    standing where it used to be
The house it was empty, the house it was dark; surely, she could not
    have left me as I was the best
I was one of a kind, I was not like the rest. Then I saw a white note,
    and here's what she wrote:
"For your very big head you need a wide door; when you had it all
    you still asked for more
I have gone to live my life and be happy on my own; I won't return,
    you're the worst man I've known"
My whole world started shaking, I must find this wench, or she'll
    spread her lies, and they'll spread like a stench
No one leaves me and stays whole, fit, and alive; the stupid woman
    thinks I'll let her survive
This time I will kill her there'll be no tomorrow; tonight, I'll get
    drunk to drown all my sorrow
Next day, I woke up with a headache and a sound in my head; what
    is this now, I felt a great dread
I couldn't figure out what this sound was about; it was a worm in my
    brain sowing strong seeds of doubt
That loud burrowing sound, I heard it again as I felt myself sinking
    into an unknown domain
It was that worm of doubt, it was living in my head, I knew it would
    not go until she is dead
She will need to die for the worm to disappear; I will kill her soon; I
    could feel she was near

Dear Doctor

Dear Doctor, now I am scared to death; did you hear him say that he
    will take my last breath
I treated him nicely look what he's done to me; maybe I should hide,
    I have nowhere to flee

How can love turn to hate, it's like lead turning to gold; I always
thought love was eternal, or so I was told
Poor Jeffry needs help; surely, he is not serious; killing people is so
strange, he must be delirious

DOC'S SCIENCE

Dear girl, I see you don't understand much of life; with the Psycho
Vulgaris you don't want a strife
I would not recommend it in any sort of way because once he goes to
war, he gets into the fey
He does not take well to rejection; he must be the winner; in the art
of killing, he's not a beginner
He played his role well until you took the bait; now run from his
wrath, I hope it's not too late
Here is an article I wrote so read it and learn; you are just one of
many to have this concern

THE ARTICLE

Some cultures that are very *macho* give a lot of space to male psychopaths to do real harm to the women in their societies. Stopping
women from educating themselves and having the freedom to live
as they see fit influence the lives of millions of women today. And
even worse, all sorts of body mutilations, forbidding women to show
their faces, *honor* killings, and such are making millions of women
suffer mainly in silence. Why in silence? Because they are afraid of
even worse punishments from their husbands, fathers, or brothers,
the very men that are meant to be on their side—what a way to live.

The role a psychopath takes on depends on his cultural and economic background, his education and his profession, his various personality traits, and how far up he is on the psychopathy scale. He will also decide which role to *play* depending on the circumstances he is in and on what goal he wants to achieve. If you are his goal, he will adapt himself to pleasing you in every way, as he is a good reader of people. The Psycho Vulgaris does not have feelings like most people; they just pretend they do until the victim lets her guard down. Dr. Robert Hare said in one of his books: "Psychopaths are social predators who charm, manipulate and ruthlessly plough their way through life, leaving a broad trail of broken hearts, shattered expectations, and empty wallets."

For instance, Ed Gacy portrayed himself as a hardworking and hard-playing but deep down softhearted and charitable man. It worked for a long time or long enough for him to kill thirty-three young men, of which twenty-seven were buried under the crawl space of his own house!

> # In the United Kingdom about 2 women are killed every week by their partners. (J. Seager)

If a psycho comes across as kind, it is only to get what he wants. He is an achiever and is solely focused on the end result and will not pay any attention to anyone's feelings or needs while getting there. He easily violates trust and is, usually, unable to sustain a relationship or faithfulness. He can be attracted to someone, but once the novelty wears off, he will harm, abuse, and hurt that same someone.

The psychopath projects his own deficiencies onto the world around him and will never be at fault. I will never forget the reaction of a psycho who crossed paths with his daughter after not seeing her for twenty years. When they saw each other, he also learned he was a grandfather, and all he had to say was that "it was not worth the bother they (the daughter and her baby) are only after my money."

Strange how he knew this when all that was said was "Hello" by both sides. Not having a close relationship with his children is one his telltale signs for psychopaths, and it may be a good idea to be aware of it. His conclusion told us all about him and his motives, which he projected onto his own child. In this same way, you will be, if in a relationship with a psycho, accused of having every one of his glaring faults.

He will show true emotion only when he feels for himself. He will feel sorry for himself if he cannot realize his plans and will cry over not getting whatever he was after.

The psychopath will seek idealized victims to shame, humiliate, and destroy them. A normal self-actualized man, for instance, will be happy he has a smart and talented girlfriend and will help her achieve her goals and share in her successes. But the psycho feels other people's success as a direct stab at himself. When other people achieve anything, his feelings of inadequacy intensify. He has the urge to destroy everyone he sees as better than himself to ease his pain, which these feelings of not being good enough carry. With psychos, the "I must have" (the first phase when you are placed on a pedestal by him) ends in "not worth having" (the second phase when he starts the devaluation process). In other words, once they achieve victory (the goal of snaring in a victim), they will immediately start to devalue the achieved goal.

Devaluation of "the chosen" one is the second phase that inevitably comes into every relationship with a psycho. This is when he shows his real nature as well as his end goal because it is by degrading you that he makes himself feel superior. Once he has achieved his goal, he will look for another victim to obtain the same high he initially had with you.

Psychopaths see themselves as superior beings in a cruel, uncaring world. They think if they don't acquire all the power, someone else will step in and obtain it. Can you imagine an environment where no one has any conscience? Conscience is what keeps the majority of people from hurting each other and is in reality the main factor that will keep people from breaking the law. The psycho has no conscience and no fear of punishment. He just cannot feel regret or remorse. He thinks it is perfectly legitimate in this *total war* they perceive around themselves to lie, cheat, steal, and even kill. They are projecting their feelings onto the world around them and consider it justified to use all they possess to outmaneuver others who are just trying to outmaneuver them. A psycho thinks everyone is just like him and will thus do to him what he can do to do to them. There is no beauty in their world and none in the psycho to project onto the world. All they see around them is what is in them, and if they feel someone has more to offer, they set out to destroy that person because they are convinced that such a person thinks they are better than him. Of course, being "better than him" is not acceptable, and the destruction of anyone they believe may be better is especially satisfying. Your average Psycho Vulgaris needs to belittle others in order to feel big himself.

The psycho needs his *victories* over others to show the world that he is better than them, that he has power over them, and, in the worst-case scenarios, that he is God, as he can determine who will live and who will die. Some psychologists and psychiatrists believe that the serial killer psycho is killing himself *symbolically* with every kill he performs. I am not so sure, just as I am not sure that they wish to be caught. *As Dennis Nilsen once said, "I was killing myself, but it was always the bystander that died."*

A Belief System or What?

ALMOST A PRAYER

Is anyone listening to me? I have something to say: I need a good woman without any delay

The one I have found is another mistake, she never really loved me, never cried for my sake

If I would say *black*, she would claim it was white; when I say go left, she will always turn right

They say that a wolf has a right to his sheep and a man has the right to all the women he can keep

I have never kept a woman, never had a wife, never nurtured a pot plant; why should I share my life

In the end, she was not that attractive, I knew her kind; she was the perfect proof that my love was blind

When I think of my life being so miserable and gory; I must have always known that God never felt sorry

God gave me no spirit; he gave me pain and a great dread; I spent my life living like the living dead

Please let me make her leave one way or another, I deserve so much more without all the bother

Why can't I just be happy and find a good mate; I must keep on trying and not leave it too late

I knew my chance for happiness was always very slim; God gave me the misery, so I will blame him

I'll watch for the full moon, and I'll howl for my pack; then someone
    will howl back, and we'll hit the track
No matter how many times I promised that I wouldn't stray, one
    moon and one howl and I'll wolf away
The night will hide me, I will never be found; I can do what I want;
    all my thoughts feel so sound!
Each time I feel elated, all happy and bright as I run with my wolf
    pack through the dense, misty night
When I get back home, I'll organize an execution; she will beg and
    cry, sensing it's the final solution
Thank you, dear devil, you have heard my prayer, you have given me
    permission to kill without care
I hope what is now will last forever and a day; I will live out my life
    in badness without any dismay
I can hurt, maim, and steal; permission given by the devil; God gave
    me free will I'll enjoy it at each level

DEAR DOCTOR

Dear Doctor, help me please I am completely confused; I already feel
    tortured, battered, and abused
Does he have two different faces, or is it a spell; will he really kill me,
    or is he just not well?
He can cross the street so he cannot be insane; he won't take pity, all
    my pleas are in vain
I can't protect myself he is bigger and stronger; I don't stand a chance,
    I won't live much longer

DOC'S SCIENCE

Dear girl, you are scared, and so you should be; he is a different animal both to you and to me

A Psycho Vulgaris will enjoy laying siege to your house; he is playing with you like a cat with a mouse

The mouse does not see it all as a game; the cat is in it for the kill, and it kills with no shame

He will keep scaring you for a very long spell, he thrives on your fear, he does not wish you well

I have written an article, so go and learn; some of it will frighten you because there is room for concern

THE ARTICLE

Like all evolved predators, the Psycho Vulgaris has developed skills for judging "other people" and deciding which ones are best to victimize. They will prey on vulnerable individuals, which represent the part of the population that does not pose a threat to him. Women and children are among the favorites, though they will also target people that are unprotected by society in principle like the homeless, drug addicts, or prostitutes. In general, they will often choose *easy* targets, meaning "people who have no strong infrastructure behind them."

Psychos hide behind a well-constructed façade of averageness that allows them to get close to people. They most often have a secret life, and their partners, even after spending years together, will wonder who this person really is and what are his secrets about. If everyone saw their true face, the face of Dorian Gray on his portrait, they would run, and the psycho would end up starved for victims.

Most humans think and feel alike, so we keep presuming that psychopaths think and feel like us as well. But they don't. Their feelings are shallow, they are only emotional when it is about them, and they are different from the average population on the inside while pretending to be like everyone else on the outside. Today, when brain imaging technology is used to map activity of the brain, it has been observed that psychopaths do not use the same parts of the brain as normal people do when processing emotional words like *love*, *death*, or similar. In most people, the right side of the brain is central in processing emotions. In psychopaths, neither side of the brain is efficient in processing emotions. These laboratory findings confirm what has been already observed in psychos, and that is as follows:

1. Their emotions are shallow.
2. Their brain does not function like the brains of the tested non-psychopaths.

Their brains are not damaged; they just function differently. If there was organic damage to their brain, they would all be making the "insanity plea" in courts and finding themselves free very quickly. Although many do plead this way hoping for less jail time, it hardly ever works.

Lycanthropy is a combination of two Greek words "wolf" and "man." It was a sixteenth-century concept that was used to explain the most brutal and senseless psychopathic murders. At the time, people believed that a lycanthrope would terrorize a village or a town, and it was considered a very big problem. The description of a lycanthrope (half wolf, half man) who is a pure predator is not easy to grasp, especially when it looks, talks, and walks like everyone else around us.

Psychopaths have another terrifying characteristic, and that is the ability to change their personality in an instant. One minute they are *in love* with you, then they hate you, then they are disinterested, then aggressive, and so on. Permanently pretending to be something they are not, they easily switch from role to role. Once the devaluation process of their victim begins, it is hard to predict their behavior. They are confusing, and even this confusion they create within their victim has a utilitarian value to the psycho. Their victims spend so much energy and time trying to understand the psycho that it leaves the victim very little time to worry about themselves. There is also the need within the victim to *make* the psycho love them. The Psycho Vulgaris does not love anyone. By permanently alternating their moods from short spells of *love* to abuse the psycho keeps the partner continuously engaged in the pursuit of love. So if you have to work too hard to be loved, something is wrong.

> In Russia 36,000 women are beaten on a daily basis by their partners or husbands according to the Russian Non-Governmental Organisations. (OMCT)

The *crueller* a history of a people and the more alienated and colder a society is, the more psychopaths it will produce. Nothing born of fear or hate produces happy, self-actualized people. Governments that rule by fear, regimes that are only money-driven, and systems where usury is a forgotten word will be a great breeding ground for people with no empathy. These kinds of *political* regimes will, for instance, promote the traits of psychopaths because it needs them to perform certain tasks, which usually have the preservation of this regime as its main goal. Warriors, the people who easily kill, are a necessity for every country that is waging a war of some kind. Armies will consist of three-quarters of normal, average men who need to be heavily indoctrinated to be able to kill the *enemy* without much after-thought and of a smaller number of psychos that don't need much prompting. Then, once the war is over, and the non-psycho soldiers come home, hundreds of thousands of men end up suffering from debilitating PTSD, and there are many of them who commit suicide. One of the saddest examples of this was with the American soldiers after the war in Vietnam. I have not heard of any of the war-waging generals who suffered the same fate after the Vietnam or any other war.

I am not sure if Nazi Germany needed psychos for their SS troops and their Concentration Camp leaders, but the leaders that created both were psychos no doubt. Stalinism must have needed psychos to work in their internal security branches like the KGB, without which it would be hard to kill millions of their own people. And today, when common decency is replaced by money, we have the psychos of Wall Street who promoted the saying "greed is good" and billionaires who pay their way out of jail. Cruelty breeds cruelty, whether long term inflicted by one's own family or by society in general. Unfortunately, it looks like we will have our lycanthropes, werewolves, vampires, and all kinds of other monsters around us for a long time to come.

The world is a beautiful and scary place, and it is a crying shame that our children are not introduced to this fact in a safe and loving environment. In the last twenty years, even well-known fables and fairy tales have been modified into boring stories full of *politically correct* messages. Our children jump from a childhood where there is no mention of evil into the real world that is in large part run by it. From the *Little Red Riding Hood* that the wolf does not wish to harm, with no preparation, they leap into the *Scream*.

Not grasping the fact that the psychos are a real threat or not even thinking that people like them exist makes the psycho's life so much easier. They are cunning, and most of us just don't expect a monster of his sort to pop up in our lives. It would be very useful if someone could think of a method of introducing scary and dangerous people to us while we are young so that the element of surprise would not be on the psycho's side. I believe we could teach about the Psycho Vulgaris just like we already teach about snakes and poisonous spiders. Armed with the tools of knowledge, we would, maybe, be able to reduce the risk of being bitten by any of them.

Who Is Wrong?

JEFFRY'S DREAM

I had a strange dream one night; I dreamt that I could fly, I felt the
 feeling of freedom as I took off for the sky
I flew around the world; with the wind I was as one; then I felt the
 sun's warmth, so I flew toward the sun
The light shining on me was now getting very strong; I must turn
 back quickly, or I won't fly for too long
"It's only a dream," I heard myself say, and right there in the air my
 wings melted away
Straight into the North Sea I went spiraling down; to my horror, I
 saw I was going to drown
It was then that I heard a heavenly knock; I heard the ringing of my
 old alarm clock
It was only a bad dream I thought pacified; I won't die; I never flew,
 and I never even tried
I reached for the light there was no light to be found; why was it
 pitch-black, am I underground?
I needed some light, there was none to be had; I was in total darkness, it was like being dead
I thought of my mother; called my brother's name nothing, but dead
 silence from the darkness came
Life is so confusing everything I know seems wrong; there is an ugly
 war on, and it will last for very long

Then I felt a change, it was something new, it was two golden stars
    coming into my view
Was I wrong again is there hope to be had; can I lose this misery,
    maybe my life doesn't have to be bad
I heard a sound in my head, and the two lights went out; it was the
    worm again, the one that sows doubt
Fear changed all my memories to fit my sick heart; though I was so
    scared, I still played my part
I sat in the dark and wearing only a frown, I remembered my prayer,
    darkness won't let me down.

DEAR DOCTOR

Dear Doctor, it is obvious that he is angry with me, he can't get out
    of the night, he needs some light to see
Oh, I do feel sorry for him his childhood was sad, his mother never
    loved him, and he didn't have a dad
All that hurt makes him swoon and he thinks he's so bad; maybe my
    love can give him what he's never had
My love can change him, he'll become a good man; to change him is
    my mission, I know
that I can

DOC'S SCIENCE

Dear girl, it is so sad to hear how you're losing the plot; he is telling
    you he'll kill you, and you think he will not
I have told you already you can't make him change; go do something
    logical, go find flowers to arrange

It is sad that he must live with all of that dread; it is even sadder that
    his solution means taking your head
Your best bet, dear girl, is to quickly disappear; you have no business
    feeling pity when your end is so near
I have written an article it may shed some light; the fact is that many
    girls went through a similar plight

THE ARTICLE

The Psycho Vulgaris knows he is not like other people; he
believes that he is right, and everyone else is wrong. He can sense
that he is not like other people even if he is not prepared to admit it.
He is sane in the legal sense of the word because he knows right from
wrong. He has free will like everyone else, but whether he chooses to
do the right thing is a different question. He feels that he is looking
through a window at the world and that he does not belong in it.
To function in the world where he is the odd one out, he must work
hard, harder than the rest because he needs to learn to mimic, learn
to manipulate, learn how to lie well, and learn how to get away with
hurting others, and he needs to learn all this before he learns to read
and write.

He does not learn from experience; has bad impulse control and
repeats the same mistakes over and over. He envies others who live
with ease, without the secret he carries. He feels the need to prove his
worth and does not understand any other category but winner and
loser. The Psycho Vulgaris is a sad individual, or is he? Dr. Martha
Stout says in her book *The Sociopath Next Door* that the most reli-
able sign, the most universal behavior of unscrupulous people, is not
directed at our fearfulness. She concludes that it is, perversely, an
appeal to our sympathy. I am convinced that this is the case in most
relationships where one individual is a psycho. The psycho abuses
and then asks for forgiveness, and the beaten-up and abused woman
feels sorry for him and keeps on giving him another chance. This

pity can and does in time turn to fear, but by then, the psycho has fully uncovered his true personality, and she looks for help, gets it or not, and she sometimes ends up dead by the hand of the man she felt so much pity for. So do not feel pity for him; try and save yourself before you attempt to save anyone else. Does the fly feel sorry for the spider just before he captures her? Probably not—our feelings are not necessarily a true reflection of what is going on around us.

Being entitled to all he considers his life unfairly difficult, and he will, naturally, feel that he was hard done by. He is mystified that one else around him seems to share this opinion; no one understands that he deserves special leniency with regard to everything and instead he gets punished for his mistakes. A psychopath will do anything he wishes, not worrying how this will affect others. They are people without a conscience. Dr. Martha Stout in the same book said that what distinguishes these people from the rest of us is an utterly empty hole in the psyche, where there should be the most evolved of all humanizing functions—the conscience.

Internally, the psycho lives in a created reality, which differs from the world we know. In his world, the victim deserves killing, and he is just dishing out justice, so naturally, he feels no remorse. The fact that his world collides with the one we are in makes him feel isolated and misunderstood. He knows he does not fit in; he has to hide who he is and feels that everything comes to others with ease, while he has to struggle. He lives in a permanent state of war with the world. I would think that is must be exhausting for the psycho. Maybe that is why quite a few of them commit suicide once they get too tired from conquering their perceived enemies that seem to be coming at them without stopping. There is not that much research done on this subject, but what is done seems to conclude that there is a high degree of suicide among them. Lisa Campbell and Anthony Beech investigated this question and, in their work, *Is There a Link Between Psychopathy and Self-Harm? A Review of the Literature*, concluded in their *Recommendations for Clinical Practice* that clinicians working with individuals who meet the criteria for psychopathy should be aware that their psychopathic traits may increase, rather than decrease their risk of self-harm. They further talk about the type of psychopath that would be more inclined to self-harm. I understand the need for this kind of awareness in one's clinical work, but my interest lies more with the victim and how to raise awareness about the danger of being involved with a psycho.

This permanent state of war he has introduced and kept in his life makes the psycho full of rage and hostility toward the world in general. He lives his life carrying the burden of a secret on top of this perceived permanent war. His secret is that he knows he is different from others, he is fully aware of all the harm he is doing to the people around him, and he knows that everything he has achieved in life is by crook. These kinds of realizations and feelings about oneself produce strong feelings of resentment. They are easily offended especially if it is hinted that they are "not as good as others." He does not have the patience to wait for the world to "discover him," so the psycho will do and say things that in his mind make him look *superior* to others. He will boast and claim he was the winner, that no one ever leaves him, that he knows best, and that he is special. He self-worships. He expects the world around him to see him in the same way. He thinks he will make people respect him if he never admits to the smallest fault. He needs to be right all the time. He insists he is always the strongest and the best. If there is a fault, it is not with him.

Everything that is wrong is done by someone else. He is never to blame for anything. He is perfect. This is exactly the opposite of the approach to personal deficiencies that a self-fulfilled mature individual would exhibit. The psychopath is above judgment. He is justified by the fact of who he is and makes no mistakes. This warped way of seeing oneself is very difficult to relate to. Over and over, he needs to prove to the world that he is perfect and always justified. He is highly defensive, and any tiny or a very mild negative comment on the psycho's account will evoke a completely disproportionate defensive reaction.

He is angry at the world and the people in it because he cannot relate to either. To add insult to injury the world around him does not seem to see or acknowledge his grandiose existence. He has no real idea of what others feel as he cannot empathize with anyone, so he sees others as objects. We don't expect ourselves to empathize with an old broom, which once broken is usually thrown away. Most people do not exhibit any special feelings of sadness when they throw away an old broom because it is an inanimate object with a specific use in everyday life. Once broken, the broom is easily replaceable with a new one. The Psycho Vulgaris cannot empathize with people, no more than we can empathize with the broom. Therefore, he sees all people as objects; everyone exists for his sake to use as he sees fit and to be discarded once there is no more use for them.

We are all here to serve his needs even at the price of enormous personal sacrifice. He cannot relate to others, so he will treat people as possessions. Psychos feel that they can and do own people; hence, they have the right to treat them however they want, and they even have the right to destroy them. Slavery has been banned everywhere, except in their world.

> **At the UN General Assembly in 2017 it was estimated that 40.3 million people are working in some form of slavery out of which 71% of modern-day slaves are women.**

The psychopath resolves differences by any means necessary. They will use verbal and physical aggression without giving it a second thought. Most of them master passive–aggressive behavior, in which case they use long silences, withhold sex and approval, and ignore a person they share a home with for months.

The Psycho Vulgaris must win every argument and will use various manipulative tactics to have the last word. For instance, they will try to shift the blame onto the other person after hurting them for not agreeing with him. For example, a psycho might say "you made me angry" or "you led me on" or "you made me do it." They can keep up the charm in a manipulative attempt to win back the favor from the person they have hurt—until they get what they are after. They often make promises that they have no intention of keeping and often resort to gaslighting or denying that they did anything wrong, attempting to make the other person start doubting themselves. The best statement I have ever heard was from a psycho who was explaining to his wife how he was being nice, and she misheard and overreacted, so he said to her, "You know what you are like. You always blow things out of proportion." This psycho has a set formula for his wife, which she is supposed to believe in and *know about herself,* so he does not need to explain much. He has made her inadequacy a fact, which she is to accept with no resistance.

British serial killer Patrick Mackay was predicted to become a serial killer by one of his doctors. Mackay identified with Hitler and liked to pose in Nazi uniforms he made himself. He confessed to have killed eleven people, including a Catholic priest with an axe, and had to have the last word at an interview, which was filmed by saying: "I shan't shed a tear. Life is full of shocks of all descriptions, and they must be faced."

Psychos are not confused; they know what they are doing when they are causing others immense harm. They don't see it as senseless harm but as justified retribution for some perceived injustice, which was done to them. Because they blame the world for their actions, they feel permanently wronged. It is because of these feelings they believe that the world owes them and should allow them greater rights than other people have. Mimicking emotions and often changing roles, they, early on in life, lose any true sense of who they are. They are afraid of being found out; they need to hide who they are because they know they would be judged harshly by society. Their actions toward others tell them so.

Even if the Psycho Vulgaris is not punished for his actions to every action, there is a reaction whether we realize it or not. In this case, I am talking about our vast and strong subconscious, which determines the level of one's self-esteem. This is not a conscious mechanism, and it happens without one being directly aware of it. I would not complicate it too much for now or use any of Freud's theories, but it is quite logical to think that if you do estimable things, including not accepting abuse, your self-esteem will grow. If you keep on bullying, cheating, threatening, blackmailing, and abusing others, your self-esteem will drop. The lower our self-esteem or the lower out self-worth, the more we need to prove ourselves as *better* than others, and the more envious we are of the people who are not like us. This is where the psychopath draws his disregard for others and his hate. He needs to crush others, thus, in his mind, proving his worth and his strength.

Is Hate Safe?

THE MAKING OF A
SERIAL KILLER

You know me, I am Jeffry, known as the Old Fart, I woke up one fine
day feeling gay and vivacious

I was ever so pleased that the hole between my ears was so very
smooth and so spacious

I had my brain removed and my heart taken out, I felt so much better, needless items no doubt

I didn't miss my brain, no one else missed my heart; I can live in
peace now like every other Old Fart

Then I saw her with a man, and lo and behold, that is when I finally
lost it or, so I was told

My eyes were blazing, and my head was pounding; the world around
me was totally confounding

The doctor came to check if my surgery had been in vain; he found
no trace of my heart, nor an ounce of my brain

But the doctor noticed a new, very serious issue; there was bad con-
tamination of the surrounding tissue

The doctor had to tell me that I was terminally ill; my chance of
survival was very close to nil

As I started to draw my final curtain; I knew that my last day was
quickly coming for certain

Apart from a pound and just a few pence, I had nothing to leave once
I transformed into past tense
No one will care when I am gone, and that wench with no pride, I
will take her with me I won't let her hide
She will beg me for mercy once I draw out my knife; I won't lose her
this time, I will take her life
Every word she ever said I felt with no heart was a lie, I knew with no
brain she was just scared to die
I craved her cries, I could smell her fear; I could hear her heartbeat,
she was painfully near
I did all I could to keep my hate going; could it be that I loved her
without even knowing?
And then something happened, I started to cry while my tragic life
passed before my one good eye
I saw my mother so cold and so distant; and in that dark night, I saw
a boy's face distorted by fright
I started shouting to the God above; I promised that if he removed
my fear, I'd live with no love
I will sacrifice my love for a life without fear; is anyone listening is
there a mighty God here
I was too young to know that a request of this level can only be personally granted by the devil
I struck a deal with the devil right then and there; I will nurture only
hate with no fear or care
I lowered my gaze to make sure it was not all a dream; everything felt
elusive, nothing was as it seemed
I started to shake, I started to shudder; I saw there was a woman my
arms, and it was my mother
You'll die now, I screamed, you were meant to be stronger; I won't let
you live for a moment longer
I will rip out you heart, I am your judge and your jury; I hated all
women with passion and fury
I watched my mother die and I started to yell; on that night I realized
I would end up in hell

Good to know, I thought; I was on the right path; I will show all
women the strength of my wrath
I won't live in anguish; I'll leave no woman intact; I will honor the
devil and honor our pact

DEAR DOCTOR

Why does Jeffry speak of hate when love is much stronger; I can't
stand this talk of killing for very much longer
He is keeping his hate going, and I am getting scared; I don't know
what to do, I am completely unprepared
I don't sleep anymore, and I don't go outside; why is he doing this
could it be his hurt pride
People come together, and they often grow apart; I have heard of
people dying from a broken heart

DOC'S SCIENCE

Dear girl, I have already told you he can't take rejection; he will never
change there is no pill or injection
You need to run and hide, and you need to do it now; he's made a
pact with the devil, he has given him a vow
He hates all women, mistrusts them, and fears them; he feels you
have betrayed him you mustn't stay near him
He's not the first, nor the last; it's not a rare occurrence; when you
first meet a man there is no assurance
Here is my article that you need to read and learn; it's your safety, not
your happiness, that's become my concern

THE ARTICLE

Quite a few male psychopaths hate all women. There are many theories as to why this is the case, but none are conclusive. Most likely, they are afraid they will be rejected by their objects of desire. They don't understand women, they fear them because they fear rejection, and they hate them because they believe that women would do to them exactly what they are doing to women. They expect to be controlled by women, robbed, used, left publicly humiliated, and then replaced by someone else. In a world that they live in, dogs eat dogs, and women eat men.

We have touched on their intense and deeply rooted feelings of fear of rejection. People with feelings of grandiosity will avoid rejection at any price, so in order not to be rejected by the object of their desire, they must have absolute power over them—in life or in death. Wifebeaters and rapists if incarcerated will reoffend regularly. Their deviant behavior can be sexualy motivated, or it can be motivated by the need for power and control. In any case, it will not stop, the psychopath will not react to therapy and will not be deterred by the fear of punishment no matter how harsh.

Harvey Glatman was a rapist and killer who hated and feared women. Women who provoked his male desires just highlighted the fact that if free they would reject any sort of an advance from him. That is why they had to be subdued, raped, and, if not compliant, killed.

In North Africa 6,000 women are genitally mutilated each day. (WHO)

In India each year 7,000 women will be murdered by their families and in-laws in disputes over dowries. (The People-Womens Chanel)

In Bolivia 17% of women aged 20 and over have experienced physical violence in the previous 12 months. (WHO)

Women in the USA experience about 4.8 million intimate partner related physical assaults and rapes each year. (USA National Centre for Injury Prevention and Control)

14,000 women die annually from domestic violence in Russia. That is 39 women a day. (Article in the *Times* by M. Roche dated March 2021)

In China over 15,000 are sold into slavery each year. (Slavery Today 2022)

In Pakistan 42% of all women accept violence as their fate. (Government study in Punjab)

Ed Kemper would often behead his victims before raping them. On one occasion, he said, "There is a lot left in a girl's body without the head and the personality is gone." Obviously, this was not a bad thing as far as Kemper was concerned because she would be quiet, not complain, and not comment. Doing away with female personality is a good thing for Kemper, and for people like him, a depersonalized body is not as scary as a living female.

Of course, not all psychopaths are serial killers, but they are all manipulative, abusive, and completely nonresponsive to human suffering. They all feel the need to control and exhibit their power over their chosen victims. Controlling a human being, just like the possession of a human being, is not acceptable and, in the end, not possible. A psychopath will inevitably lose control over another human being in various ways. The victim will either successfully run away, the psycho will be locked up long enough for his victim to flee, or he will kill her rather than let her go and be left with feelings of rejection and worthlessness.

David Berkowitz, son of Sam, hated all women and said in an interview that he blamed women for everything because all evil things that have happened in the world somehow go back to women.

It was Eve, after all, who offered Adam the forbidden fruit as it is said in Judeo Christianity. In the Muslim world, by large, females must be considered irresponsible by nature because men have taken on themselves to protect their chastity by imposing various measures, by which they will *make* the women in their society live virtuously. In Africa, men have imposed genital mutilation to keep their women sexually subdued. So in a world of this kind, it is not difficult for the Psycho Vulgaris to rationalize and to hate all women.

It is quite common among them to blame it all on their mother. The more psychotherapy they undergo, the more knowledge they gain about how to present themselves as victims of *motherly* abuse, thinking that their story should be enough to justify their heinous acts toward women. Most people are not convinced by their stories, and if they were abused, there is no reason to pass on the abuse. Most victims of motherly abuse do not continue to abuse other people. Again, the psycho chooses what it is he wishes to do, and then he does it while knowing it is wrong and then thinks he should get away with it. There are many theories about the harm that dominant mothers cause to their male offspring. Men seem to be more affected by these mothers than women possibly because men presume that their role in the family and society in general should be dominant.

According to the *Oxford English Dictionary*, the English word *misogyny* was coined in the middle of the seventeenth century from the Greek *misos*, "hatred" + *gunē*, "woman." Hatred or contempt of women is the kind of sexism that gives women a lower social status compared to men. It is an attitude found in patriarchal societies and is still widespread today. It has been practiced for thousands of years and is reflected in art, literature, mythology, and philosophy, as well as in various religions.

Misogyny in its extreme form legitimizes violence against *un-obedient* women or women in general. It often manifests through sexual harassment and various techniques aimed at controlling women and by legally or socially excluding women from the rights that are widespread among men. The notion that *good* women accept a lower social status and that the ones who think they have the same rights are *shrews* and need to be tamed is still strong in our so-called civilized societies today. The fact that women are less paid for same jobs than men and that they are less voted into roles that carry power or a high degree of responsibility are just some of the indicators that show that patriarchal values are still dominant. Misogyny can be understood both as an attitude held by individual men and widespread cultural custom or system.

When a psycho is rejected by a woman or even if there is a hint of possible rejection, in his mind, he is being rejected by the lowest of the low that is nothing but an object of his sexual desire. She can be just an object to exercise his power or just a *thing* to be used for sex, but in any case, she is an object to use and destroy at will. Since he is perfect and she is nothing, killing her is no big deal. They deserve it, and he is just dishing out justice. In his mind, he is like all other men, just a bit more intense.

Who Are You?

THE CHAMELEON

I am the Chameleon; I can play any role from your dream, it's because
    I am no one, I am not who I seem
I am the lover, the meek grandad, the killer with no shame; if you
    enter my world, you will play my game

> **Although stalking is a gender neutral crime most (78%) stalking victims are female and most stalking perpetrators (87%) are male. (National Institute of Justice–Centers for Disease Control and Prevention)**

Monday

She wanted a rouge, and a rouge is what I played; her name was
    Susanne, and she left me betrayed
She didn't take long to change her dumb mind, just because she left
    all her children behind

One day I watched her as she opened her front door; then I pushed
her in, and she fell on the floor
She tried to get up, but I was much stronger: now Susanne can't miss
me since she's breathing no longer
I felt happy and strong when I went home on that day; I got rid of
that hussy without any delay

Tuesday

One spring, sunny Tuesday, I met Sarah Lee; the strong and the silent
type is what she wanted from me
I'll be strong and silent, I can accommodate; I can always change my
spots, they all take the bait
One morning she asked me to go as it was her house; she said I stole
and lied and was just a louse
I will burn your house; it will go up in a blaze, and I'll watch you die
through the thick smoke and haze
I went home, again, all happy and pleased 'cause in the midst of that
smoke I never once sneezed

Wednesday

On one summer Wednesday, I went for a long walk, when I met
Josephine, who adored to talk
She was after a sensitive man with very deep emotions; she'll get what
she wants with no magic potions
In a few weeks, she said that she must depart because I have shallow
emotions and I have no heart
She is still with me though she rushed, and she hurried; she's dead in
my basement all peaceful and buried
I fondly remember how well I ate that night; it must have been the
digging that caused my appetite

Thursday

Thursday came on a lip year as it was bound to do; I went to the
movies where I met pretty Prue
Prudence did not want a man; she wanted a boy; I had no problem
adapting I will be her toy
A fortnight went by, I thought it may be love; then Prue made a run
for it, tried to fly off like a dove
Again, I had to do what the devil intended; I whipped old Prue to
death as she had offended
I felt very lucky that Thursday, so I went to play poker, won a bit of
money thanks to my extra Joker

Friday

I got a hunch on a Friday to go to the store, and lo and behold, I then
met Pussy Galore
Pussy was a happy girl, and she loved to play; with no further com-
plications, we just hit the hay
She wanted a real man all hairy and sweaty; I did not have to change
much because I smelled like a Yeti
I didn't think twice, chose a knife with a sharp blade; then and there,
in an instant, Pussy's future was made
As she fell to the ground, I was thinking of gravity and how it only
takes over when they finish with me

Saturday

Dawn was looking for a man who was a hardened criminal; a simple
role for me, as the change was minimal
She spent Saturday with me, and as she looked me in the eye, I think
she knew then she was going to die
I will kill her now as she saw right through me; I'll remain an enigma
as the rest never knew me
I hung her by her neck till she could wiggle no more, then I cut the
rope and left her on the floor

I felt strong and mighty like a god on the ground; I was a bit disap-
    pointed a good woman can't be found

Sunday

It was Sunday now, and I felt the sun burn, then I remembered the
    one that would never return
I remember asking her what she wanted me to be; she said it was a
    silly question because all I can offer is me
I knew where she lived, and I watched her every day; and when I
    followed her, it felt like stalking prey
I watched her every move; I always knew where she was; not being
    seen while watching gave me a buzz
I know she is scared; I enjoy all her fear; I am big, and I'm strong, and
    I will always be near

DEAR DOCTOR

One Sunday, he made me stop in my track's dead, I saw him in front
    of me and here is what I said
I said, "Good morning, dear stalker, nice to see you here"; I could feel
    your presence, I know when you are near
By playing this strange game, you have entered my head; is it love
    you are after, or do you wish me dead
You are sending me a message, but it is not clear; what is it you want
    my fancy or my fear
I look for you under the stairs and under my bed; I wonder by which
    method will you make me dead
Are you going to strangle me, will you watch me squirm, or will you
    just crush me as you would a worm
Have you considered the possibility of using the knife; it is a popular
    tool when it comes to taking life

You could slit my throat or stab me to death and then fully enjoy my
    last gargling breath
Forgive if I feel I need police protection if all you are doing comes
    from your true affection
Sometimes I do doubt that this is all about me: could be an attempt
    to rule your own destiny?
Can it be that I'll die because of your resolution to determine the
    date of your own execution
It may not be personal, so I'll stop asking why; I am just a means, one
    way for you to die
You need to be punished, you think dying is fine; you can't take your
    own life, so you will take mine
But what about me, I would still like some life; okay, I'll stop talking
    now no need to cause strife
Sometimes I can't move; it's like there's lead in my veins; how can this
    be good for you, what would be your gains
I scream when I am scared looking into the abyss; all my screams stay
    inside of me, it is my freedom I miss
If nobody saves me, I will need a resurrection; I'll have to look for the
    law, they might give me some protection

DOC'S SCIENCE

All these lovely ladies, what a shame, what a sin; because of his evil
    nature, he has done them all in
They did nothing wrong just wanted a normal life; all he saw was
    rejection, claimed he couldn't find a wife
Was it a wife he wanted, or did he just want to kill; on a scale of hap-
    piness, his result would be nil
Mind the flatterers and the slick ones, stay away from his rage; he will
    say he is sorry, but he's not by this stage
When you see his true face, he'll not go back to being nice; you will
    now start to suffer from his each and every vice

There is a whole science that deals with people like him; they are
      trying to stop him from hurting women on a whim
My point is, dear girl, you must run and run very fast; this is not a
      happy friendship, it's his hate that will last
Do not count on anyone including the police force; first run and
      hide, and then worry about remorse
Make this, my dear girl, your only priority for now; first you need to
      save your life, then you'll think of what and how
I have written an article just to show you it's no game; bad people are
      out to hurt, and they'll kill without shame

THE ARTICLE

When talking about the Psycho Vulgaris, it is important to say
that we can all feel anger, have low self-esteem, tell a lie, wish to control the people around us, or feel bored. The Psycho Vulgaris has all
these feelings with the exception that his emotions are much more
intense than ours. It is like having a glass of wine with dinner as
opposed to being a raging alcoholic. Also, the difference between
us and them is in what they don't feel, and we do, like remorse or
empathy or even fear.

Serial killers are on the very high end of the scale of psychopathy. We can say that not all psychopaths are serial killers, but all serial
killers are psychopaths. Serial killing is the rarest form of homicide.
To earn the status of a serial killer, a person must kill three or more
individuals with a *cooling off* period between the murders.

There are various categorizations of serial killers, of which one
is the division between the *organized* and *disorganized* serial killers.

Organized serial killers plan their attacks, often stalk their victims, have a kill kit to hand, usually have an average or above-average
intelligence, can hold down a good job, can have relationships, can
be charming, etc. Ted Bundy was one of these serial killers.

The disorganized serial killer is unkempt, has employment issues, is a loner without any relationships, and has no social skills and a lack of planning, and they don't bother with the cleanup of the murder scene. Most often, their victims are unknown to them, and apart from psychopathy, they often struggle with other mental health issues. Son of Sam was a disorganized serial killer.

The above two categories are based on the characteristics of execution, not on the psycho's motives for killing. The FBI has added another category to the two above categories, and that is the medical serial killer. This category refers to mainly doctors and nurses exercising their power over life and death and killing their patients for so-called humane reasons, for instance, to stop their suffering.

There is another division that is based on the serial killer's motivation. This categorization considers six main types of motives, which prompt serial killers into action.

The *Visionary Killer* is often psychotic and suffers from delusions and hallucinations. They usually pick random targets and lack planning. They believe they are being commanded to kill and make little if any effort to hide their crimes. For instance, they can feel ordered to sacrifice a certain amount of people to stop some big disaster. They think they are saving humanity through their actions and may expect gratitude for their actions.

The *Mission-orientated* serial killer is organized, plans his crimes, and does not suffer from psychosis. These killers target a specific group of people; they kill quickly and avoid close contact with their victims. They prefer to use guns. Their missions can be, for instance, to "rid the world of prostitutes." So they also consider that they are doing humanity a favor.

Then, there is the *Lust* serial killer who rapes, tortures, and mutilates because this gives him sexual gratification. These killers fantasize about violence and find it difficult to control their impulses. They usually kill their victims to keep themselves from being found out. They prefer close contact with their victims and will use a knife or hands instead of a gun.

The *Thrill* serial killer gets a thrill out of killing. For instance, hunting their victim or just seeing their victim's terror will give them an adrenaline rush. These killers often feel inadequate and powerless and lose all interest once their victim is dead because exercising power over a dead person is not very gratifying. These kinds of killers choose a group, and they don't necessarily choose the individual victim. They will target the so-called socially marginalized groups, the people whom societies will consider as outcasts like the homeless, prostitutes, drug addicts, etc.

The *Comfort* killer kills for money and wealth. These killers are often females, but most of these types of serial killers are still men. They often use poison to kill their victims. They avoid close contact. Their murders are means to an end, and they don't especially enjoy committing them. They can wait for a long time from one kill to the next and are often described as black widows or black widowers.

The *Power/Control* killers seek to establish absolute power over their victim. They have an exceptionally strong feeling of inadequacy and are scared of rejection, which would confirm this inadequacy. They need to dominate their victims and are organized and patient. They often sexually assault their victims, but sex in this case is not the goal; rather, it is the exercise of power.

In life, we usually find mixed categories of serial killers, and the categories often overlap. They can have mainly the characteristics of one group of serial killers with elements from any other group.

As I have briefly mentioned, serial killers are a combination of genetics and upbringing. They are gradually formed as they mature when they can realize their ideation of domination or killing of their perspective victims. There are certain signs that are visible in children and teenagers, which point to a possible psychopath or even a serial killer. These signs are in very wide categories the exhibiting of antisocial tendencies, tendencies toward arson, torturing small animals, unhealthy family life, childhood abuse, and substance abuse.

The age when serial killers start to realize their fantasy life is usually anywhere between twenty-five and forty-five years of age. There are exceptions, of course, where the serial killer has had his first victim by the age of eighteen or even younger.

While interesting reading, this is not an exact science. It is the commonsense directions that can maybe help save a few lives, suggestions like do not trust strangers straight away and be curious about a person as to his background, achievements, family, etc. I would add meeting his friends and parents before getting seriously involved with anyone. Be aware of your own vulnerabilities; for instance, do you have a strong mothering instinct he can play on? Or are you inclined to protect the underdog without really knowing who you are dealing with? Are you lonely enough to accept anyone's company? Is everything he says too in tune with your own opinions? Are you being love-bombed like never before? Does he sound too good to be true? Also, you should stay away from risky behaviors like hitchhiking or accepting rides or visits from people you do not know, don't accept to go anywhere with strangers, and just have a general awareness that very bad people exist and do not necessarily live somewhere else. Trust your gut feeling. Avoid offering or helping strangers yourself, and always call the appropriate authorities if someone needs help.

All serial killers are psychopaths. They all have certain common characteristic regardless of how they chose to live. Apart from not having empathy or conscience, lying without a problem, blaming the world for what they do, impulsivity, lack of fear, stealing often, or living by exploiting others, they have some common telltale signs. Psychopaths will rarely know details about their own children, i.e., they lack connection with their own children. They come across as superficial and glib and very often have a parallel secret life. They have no sense of responsibility, cheat, and often indulge in substance abuse. They are quite often *bored* and will thus indulge in risky activities like gambling, driving too fast, etc. Do not let them draw you into this world. All in all, Psycho Vulgaris is not the kind of man who will have your back or stay faithful, and he will abuse you in every possible way that he can. If he disappears for long periods of time, if he dislikes all your friends, if he thinks you should not be seeing your family, if he is moody, if he has to win every argument, if you keep on catching him in lies, if he is vague about his family and childhood, or if he is a complete loner with no friends, I would be worried.

What Law and Order?

Dear Doctor

Dear Doctor, I was thinking of my stalker and the last time we met;
    I know he's a killer; he just hasn't killed me yet
I can't run, I can't hide, and I don't really want to; I looked for the
    police, hoping there was something they'd do
One day, while still looking, I stumbled upon a policeman; he lis-
    tened to my tale, said he would do what he can
First, he said, he would need to write down all of my sad story; the
    more details the better, he hoped they'd be gory
Then, the law said he'll have to consult his beloved superior as I
    might have a motive that may be ulterior
Once the law makes sure there is a formal case to be had, they will
    talk to my stalker who may not be all bad
They said it was questionable if he'll harm me in any way; he has not
    killed me yet, and I can't prove that he may
After all, they must be careful because all true crime situations are
    bound to have serious financial implications
The fact that he has a criminal history may add to the danger; after
    all, I had no business talking to a stranger
They knew I paid tax, hence the granted attention; but if my time
    has come, I'll need divine intervention
They will have to consider if his childhood was blue; in which case
    the Social Services will know what to do

They said that he may suffer from a mental disorder, which would
    grant them powerless to uphold law and order
If he was the victim of a historic chronology, intervening would be
    wrong, they'd have to give him an apology
They stated that he will not be the hero that they'll get him when he
    kills me since their tolerance is Zero!
While listening to the law I saw a spark in Jeffry's eye, I saw there was
    no protection, I knew I would die

Doc's science

Dear girl, you've made me sad as it could be a premonition; he is
    heading for the end and for your demolition
Our police always wait for the crime to be committed, they don't do
    prevention, from our law that's omitted
You got a restraining order, which he happily broke; no one did a
    thing about it, it's almost a joke
I told you to run and hide, your protection is up to you; I wrote you
    an article to read, that is all I could do

The article

The universal declaration of human rights in Article 2 states,
"Everyone is entitled to all the rights and freedoms set forth in this
declaration, without distinction of any kind, such as race, colour,
sex, language, religion, political or other opinion, national or social
origin, property, birth, or other status."

What does reality say to this wonderful thought? It says that,
as always, we all have the same rights, except that some people have
more rights than others. There seems to be an unwritten general

agreement in every society about who should be protected and who has less rights to protection. For instance, it is not uncommon in the West that criminals regularly get more jail time for a bank robbery than for rape or even murder. Who is being protected in this case? The banks and the banking industry and capital, of course.

The legal concept of *due diligence* describes the minimum acceptable level of effort that a state must undertake to fulfill its responsibility to protect individuals from abuse of their basic rights. Due diligence includes taking effective steps to prevent abuse, to investigate it when it does occur, and to bring the perpetrator to justice in a fair trial. Justice is meant to be upheld without any discrimination.

Data from the Crime Survey of England and Wales shows up to 700,000 women are stalked each year (British Crime Survey 2006). Maybe the worst of all is the fact that 85 percent of female victims sought help four to five times on average from professionals in the year before they got effective help.

74% of Stalking Victims are between the ages of 18 and 39

87% of stalkers identified by their victims were men

80% of restraining orders are violated by the offender

77% of stalking victims are stalked by someone they know

59% of female victims are stalked by intimates or x-intimates (husband, lover, boyfriend)

81% of women who are stalked by a current or a former intimate are also physically assaulted by the same person

31% of women who are stalked by a current or a former intimate are also sexually assaulted by the same person.

(National Institute of Justice–Centers for Disease Control and Prevention USA 2022)

The percentages listed above are averages for the Western world and differ very little from country to country. Stalking behavior has been identified in nine out of ten murders studied by criminologists as part of research examining a link between the two crimes. The six-month study by the University of Gloucestershire found stalking was present in 94 percent of the 358 cases of criminal homicides they looked at. Surveillance activity, including covert watching, was recorded 63 percent of the time. So when the police tell you that they cannot do anything about a stalker, that you need to be hurt before they react, that they are not here to prevent crimes, etc. they are not exercising due diligence.

Blaming the victim is a common occurrence when it comes to female victims in our so-called *civilized* society. It is amazing how very many people will accept that this happens, but it always happens somewhere else. We presume it is reserved for the so-called third-world countries, the *less fortunate* and less enlightened part of the world. Rape victims should not have worn the short skirt, giving directions to someone has been interpreted as talking to strangers, walking on your own after dark is inviting trouble, etc. As far as crime prevention is concerned, if the police got an inkling that someone is preparing to rob a bank, they would immediately *react*. They would stop the bank from being robbed if they were warned that a bank robbery was being planned and by whom. So how can this be in a just world? They cannot react when a stalker is concerned but can if money is about to go missing. It is strange when we all know that money can and is regularly printed and that we have no way of *resurrecting* a human once life is lost.

Psychopaths will play on these misconceptions while manipulating the police, which is populated by men or by women who quite often identify with men in order to get ahead in the police force. All this results in women getting extraordinarily little assistance while being stalked. It is surprising in how many countries (England being one of them), the police force is only there to react to a crime committed, and they will not get involved in the prevention of a crime, or, better said, they will not get involved in the prevention of some crimes.

Psychopaths can allow you, their possession, happiness only through themselves. If you leave him, he loses all power, which is why he stalks. There is a general misconception that stalking is about the lack of willingness to let go of love. On the contrary, it is about anger, which comes from losing power over a victim. It is an attempt to regain that power. Leaving the psycho is an extremely dangerous moment precisely for this reason, and unfortunately, most murders are committed during the initial breakaway period. If you are in this situation, plan, ask centers for battered women for help with your getaway, and try and leave when he is not around; change your phone number once you escape, and try and settle in a new place without telling too many people of your new address so that it may stay hidden from the psycho.

So I think we can confidently say that "zero tolerance" to crime against women is applied from time to time, prevention of crime is in the victim's hands, and that "crime" in this case has a very fluid meaning.

Are Feelings the Truth?

LIFE OR DEATH OR SOMETHING IN BETWEEN

One morning I tried to sit up in my bed wondering if I was alive, or
did I maybe wake up dead
The question is, if I died, was it of natural causes; or did I die of an
illness that had no good prognoses
I wondered if I died was my funeral sad; where was my grave, and
were there drinks to be had
Then I got confused because I could wiggle my toes; if I am still alive,
where are the worries and woes
I wanted a smoke, but I had no match, my right foot was itching, but
I could not move to scratch
I once had a love, was it up in the mountain; I felt an awful thirst,
but there was no fountain
I watched her as her life drained from her familiar face while I held
her tightly in my deadly embrace
I was not in a coffin, I saw I was in a big bed; I must be alive then, I
did not wake up dead
Oh, that dreaded itch it just won't go away; I tried to move both
hands, neither hand would obey
My throat felt so dry, I needed a drink; where could I go get one, it
was too hard to think

Not an inch had I moved, was I held by a bracket? I took me a while
to see I was in a straitjacket

DOC'S SCIENCE

My friend is no more, she feels no more stress, six feet under is now
her permanent address
I was scared he would kill her, and she was scared too; read all of our
writing so it doesn't happen to you
Women are his pray, he won't pick on a strong man; he is physically
stronger, she can't do what he can
It is a sad, sad world when no help is at hand; 50,000 dead ladies a
year is very hard to understand
There are big words everywhere but a pitiful lack of action; the ladies
are disappearing, they are going by subtraction
All this means for certain that very few people care; if lawmakers
really cared, the Vulgaris wouldn't dare

THE ARTICLE

What does a psycho feel? What kind of an existence is it? Are
they insane? Watching a psycho live like a spider in human society
is not even entertaining. Their natural habitat should be jail, where
they belong on many levels. It is interesting that today in the Western
world, about 50 percent of inmates in any prison are psychopaths.
Going through people's lives only to rob, pillage, and destroy or
using all one's capacity to manipulate and steal is truly a miserable
existence.

They have a sense of grandiosity and are convinced they know
more than other people; they have no remorse and no mercy. They

attach imaginary importance to themselves, which no one else can see and have a baseless feeling of always being the winner. They are a bit like the blowfish. The blowfish is a little fish that blows itself up to a few times its normal size when it wants to seem stronger and bigger. In the fish world, this is natural and done only in the face of an enemy when the fish feels threatened.

The Psycho Vulgaris blows himself up and tries to maintain this grandiose state forever. He is pathetic when his bubble bursts because he shrinks back to what he is: a quivering, little man with not much of anything of value. To be perceived as a *big man* and to keep this charade going, he will do anything because, once deflated, everyone can see what a *tiny fish* he is.

The Psycho Vulgaris does not see himself as insane, he knows what he is doing, he knows it is not right, and he just does not care. He is highly manipulative toward everyone without exception and will stoop as low as need be to win a war he has waged on humanity. Often, his formative years are marked by incredibly cruel and negligent parents. In about two-thirds of known psychopathy cases, psychiatry has determined that the Psycho Vulgaris endured horrific abuse. That leaves one-third of them without any glaring *abnormalities* in their childhood that still turn to killing, torture, and rape. This would indicate a combination of nurture and nature, which when *just right* will produce a psychopath.

Though the Psycho Vulgaris can be intelligent, his emotional development is warped and stunned in its growth in part due to his lack of mentioned emotional components and sometimes also by a cruel set of circumstances in his formative years. He can learn and become an expert in some field but what he cannot do is fix his emotions. The main emotion that they lack is empathy. This does not mean that everyone with a sad childhood is a psycho; on the contrary, truly good and strong people very often overcome their childhood unhappiness. It is the weak links among us with underlining tendencies toward psychopathy that an unhappy set of circumstances break and deform into psychos.

H. Cleckley in his book, *The Mask of Sanity*, said, "It must be remembered that even the most severely and obviously disabled psychopath presents a technical appearance of sanity." We believe this to be true due to the *chameleon* capacity they all possess, so they easily mimic other people's behaviors.

Knowing people and which buttons to press is the main condition of manipulating others. If the psycho did not learn to fit in and if the was not a good liar and manipulator, how could he become a serial anything? To be a serial killer, a mass murderer, or a serial rapist apart from the abovenamed characteristics, the Psycho Vulgaris must have another necessary trait. For his kind of existence, he needs to be fearless.

Many studies have confirmed that psychos have a higher threshold for fear than the average man. This allows them to undertake all sorts of actions that normal people may think of but would never turn into reality. Not fearing the consequences of their behavior allows them to continually harm one person, after another. If the Psycho Vulgaris felt fear, he would not be able to play out various harmful scenarios and be able to repeat them over and over. The fearless Psycho Vulgaris is not afraid to undertake whatever he deems necessary to obtain one of his *victories* over someone. As I mentioned earlier, their brains are wired differently to most other people's brains, and it is probably this wiring that makes them fearless. It could also be the reason why they do not change. Strangely enough, they are not good soldiers as they hate authority and never cooperate with a group. They take unnecessary risks, thus risking the lives of the soldiers around them.

There are many professions, which should have an expert at their entrance exams to weed out the psychos, for instance, nuclear power stations, police, army, anyone doing prison work, teachers and any profession that brings them in close contact with children, and many more. Politicians should also be checked for this trait, as they are given a huge responsibility and have enormous room for manipulation at the expense, sometimes, of a whole nation.

Psychologist and writer Kevin Dutton classified jobs preferred by psychopaths from 1 to 10:

10. *Civil Servant*—Dutton ranks working in the *Home Office* as the tenth most popular career choice for psychopaths. Indeed, in 1982, a scientific officer at the Home Office wrote a proposal, uncovered by the *BBC*, which suggested that in the event of a nuclear disaster, police should consider recruiting psychopaths to help keep order.

9. *Chef*—they thrive in chaos, which is too often present in kitchens; maybe for this reason, the job of head chef might appeal to a psychopath.

8. *Clergy*—the belief that they are acting in accordance with God's laws legitimizes their actions; and as a priest, they will gain access to a congregation, which is always full of people whom they might be able to both manipulate and control.

7. *Police*—remaining cool and calm under pressure when operating in a highly dangerous and stressful environment could only ever be an asset for a policeman or woman. (I would add that, unfortunately, there is the other side to this picture. Today [2022], more than 600 members of the police force in the UK are being investigated for sexual and other offenses.)

6. *Journalist*—an effective journalist needs to be charming, focused, mindful, and then ruthless. How else to extract the information required from sources reluctant to relinquish it?

5. *Surgeon*—is there a more stressful job than that of a surgeon? The person whose accuracy needs to be so acute that a mere moment's distraction could effectively end the life of another human being. In 2015, the Royal College of Surgeons conducted *a study* entitled *A Stressful Job: Are Surgeons Psychopaths?*, and the results revealed that consultants at teaching hospitals scored higher on the psychopathic scale than members of the general public.

4. *Salesperson*—the dogged desire to get ahead. Telling lies to promote personal gain is often the characteristic of an unethical salesperson; it is a tactic often used by psychopaths.

3. *Media*—psychopaths with their cool, calm, and collected approach would be likely to perform well there too.

2. *Lawyer*—a bit like journalists, lawyers must be able to coax and cajole. They'd need to do this to win over clients and later convince a jury. Many lawyers will stick to unethical practices for this reason.

1. *CEO*—psychopaths not only operate well in chaos, but sometimes, they strive to create it. Why? It makes them look good to succeed when those around them seemed destined to fail.

I think that having psychos as police officers, journalists, clergy, etc. is not good. Performing under pressure surely cannot beat the lying, manipulation, bullying, sex crimes, and other horrors these people are inclined to commit. It does, however, show how society promotes certain common traits of psychopaths, but it also explains why less and less people trust politicians, CEOs, journalists, the clergy, and the police. I believe that once the psychopath becomes prevalent in a certain kind of position, that position loses respect within the community. I was always fascinated by the stupidity of most journalists that follow sensationalism rather than the truth because is it such a reputation wrecker. Or how about the lying politicians who urge people to vote not realizing that people get sick and tired of trying to figure out which one is the least of the liars. Psychopathy is a mental disorder, not a characteristic that should be enhancing anyone's career prospects.

So why don't we put them in insane asylums once we figure them out? Because insane asylums are hospitals, and people are placed into them with the goal of administering some form of therapy, which is eventually going to make them well again and fit to be released into society. Remember, they do not change, nor do they react to psychotherapy of any kind. They use it to manipulate the therapists, to say what the parole board wishes to hear, and to attract new victims once they are let out. An illustration of how easily they can dupe psychiatrists was executed by a known serial killer, Ed Kemper.

In their attempt to re-evaluate Ed Kemper's state of mind, two doctors did a series of tests and interviews with him and decided that the therapy had worked. They decided that now he was *safe* to be let out, and all the while that this was going on, Ed Kemper had the head of one of his victims in the trunk of his car parked outside of the doctor's office. He fooled them by learning what to do and say from his therapy sessions.

There is not one authentic case of a *cured* psychopath anywhere in the world, which is why jail is the best place for them. But new Psychos Vulgaris are born all the time, and we cannot know who will offend until they do. It seems it takes a long time to catch them, an even longer time to recognize them. The majority will walk free.

For now, the only thing we can do is raise awareness so that as many people as possible learn to be aware of their dark existence and to try and recognize them for who they are and not get involved with them. If you are already involved, you need to understand that you will not change him. No one needs that kind of a spider in their life, so run wisely, and try and get help.

Epilogue

How many hundreds of thousands of women suffer and are killed by the people closest to them in one year? To this, you can add all the abused children and all those nameless whom we, as humans, victimize and just leave behind.

I don't know what this number would be, and I cannot even begin to work it out. How often do we even think of those who are all around us and who live in poverty, who are alone and old, who live with disabling illnesses, and who are being abused in some way right this minute?

No doubt, we live surrounded by a startling number of unhappy and tortured people. We can all help a little bit, which is better than nothing but by no means enough. I am sure I won't see a significant change in my lifetime, so I can only hope that every tortured soul will be able to swim to a better shore one day.

DOES DEATH EXIST?

I woke up from a deep sleep, my watch said it was eleven; I was not
   sure where I was, but hoped I was heaven

I saw a swing on the moon and reached for the nearest star; then I
   heard a beautiful voice, and the voice came from afar

"You're on the road to salvation," it said, "you are not here, nor there
   all you need to do is be still and say a little prayer"

I prayed and was still till I could be still no more; I had to ask a few
   questions while in between the after and before

I asked who knew when things were meant to be, who understood
   love, and what was the Great Mystery

I asked if the Grim Reaper existed and was the little Cupid real; can
   a broken heart mend, does a hurt soul ever heal

The voice chuckled and said that being curious if fine and that I'll
   answer my own questions when I learn about Time

I laid my head on a cloud and put one foot on a star, I loved listening
   to stories, and this will be the best one by far

I heard a chair being pulled up and water poured into a glass, then
   someone blew their nose, and so the story goes:

The Master of Time was a good-natured fellow; from the very begin-
   ning, he was seen as being amicable and mellow

It remains a great wonder how he acquired such a bad reputation
   during his brief affiliation with the human nation

All he attempted to do was teach; to help humans understand that
   there is a set plan, which is called the Grand Plan

The Grand Plan is all that is meant to be, everything is set out with
   precision, so there's no room for random decision

Sadly, quite often things were not all that smooth, the human race
   was self-centered and even uncouth

People pray to God to make their wishes come true, but when their
   turn comes, they find something else to do

They must finish the book, first; go quench their thirst, first; take a
   vacation, decide on their future vocation

The Master of time stressed, and all better believe it if a prayer is
    about to be granted, people can only take it, or leave it
If everyone was free to decide, there on the spot, whether the time is
    convenient to accept God's grace or not
The Grand Plan would be ruined, and chaos would reign; and chaos
    is the entrance to the devil's domain
Humans seem quite oblivious to how complicated and serious it is to
    set up all the elements to present the final circumstance
The Master felt there was no gratitude, just the tiresome explaining
    and permanent human nitpicking and complaining
He found working with humans irritating, there was no job satisfac-
    tion; for him, it had all lost its power of attraction
He remembered the time when the "Grim Reaper" went to work
    with a smile, he tried explaining death to humans for a long
    while
He tried to tell them he is taking them to a better place; a proposi-
    tion, he reckoned, they would gladly embrace
To his great surprise, all he came upon was resistance, so after trying
    for a few centuries, he stopped offering assistance
Interacting with humans, as things now seem, resulted in him being
    called the Grim Reaper though he wasn't really grim
He also remembered when little Cupid quit; the little cherub plucked
    up his courage and said to God that was it!
He said people pray for love and, once they get it, they start acting
    stupid; then they lose all they had and blame it on Cupid
God saw his dismay and told him that he may keep his distance and
    his path narrow but still do the job by using an arrow
They agreed that wasting their efforts was a big shame; instead of
    gaining wisdom, humans look for who to blame
The voice chuckled and said, "It's time for it to depart"; it said it will
    return once I had a good look into my heart
It said, "Listen to your heart, don't attempt to use your brain, matters
    of the heart belong to a much different domain"
You can use your brain to build the highest dome, but no one can
    think their way to love, or think a house into a home

I was then told I was dead but not to be upset; death is just a new
     door opening, and nothing has ended yet
I am on my heavenly journey, I have gone part of the way; I don't
     know where I'll be next or how long I will stay

The End

About the Author

Victoria Wolf was born in 1952. Her father was an ambassador. She grew up in Washington, District of Columbia, and lived in Moscow, Belgrade, and Switzerland. She has been in England for about thirty-five years. She has a degree in psychology and has had about eight translations published in Serbian from English and one from Japanese. She helped publish her father's memoir, *The Moscow Diary*, which became a world bestseller and was translated into seventeen languages. She has a husband, a son, and a daughter-in-law, two amazing granddaughters, and five cats and lives in a village about twenty miles from London.